HORRID HENRY

HOLIDAY HORRORS

FRANCESCA SIMON

FRANCESCA SIMON SPENT HER CHILDHOOD ON THE BEACH IN CALIFORNIA AND STARTED WRITING STORIES AT THE AGE OF EIGHT. SHE WROTE HER FIRST HORRID HENRY BOOK IN 1994. HORRID HENRY HAS GONE ON TO CONQUER THE GLOBE; HIS ADVENTURES HAVE SOLD MILLIONS OF COPIES WORLDWIDE.

FRANCESCA HAS WON THE CHILDREN'S BOOK OF THE YEAR AWARD AND IN 2009 WAS AWARDED A GOLD BLUE PETER BADGE. SHE WAS ALSO A TRUSTEE OF THE WORLD BOOK DAY CHARITY FOR SIX YEARS.

FRANCESCA LIVES IN NORTH LONDON WITH HER FAMILY.

WWW.FRANCESCASIMON.COM WWW.HORRIDHENRY.CO.UK @SIMON_FRANCESCA

TONY ROSS

TONY ROSS WAS BORN IN LONDON AND STUDIED AT THE LIVERPOOL SCHOOL OF ART AND DESIGN. HE HAS WORKED AS A CARTOONIST, A GRAPHIC DESIGNER, AN ADVERTISING ART DIRECTOR AND A UNIVERSITY LECTURER.

TONY IS ONE OF THE MOST POPULAR AND SUCCESSFUL CHILDREN'S ILLUSTRATORS OF ALL TIME, BEST KNOWN FOR ILLUSTRATING HORRID HENRY AND THE WORKS OF DAVID WALLIAMS, AS WELL AS HIS OWN HUGELY POPULAR SERIES, THE LITTLE PRINCESS. HE LIVES IN MACCLESFIELD.

HORRID HENRY
HOLIDAY HORRORS

FRANCESCA SIMON

ILLUSTRATED BY TONY ROSS

Orion

ORION CHILDREN'S BOOKS

Stories first published in "Horrid Henry: Monster Movie",
"Horrid Henry: Krazy Ketchup", "Horrid Henry: Up, Up and Away", "Horrid
Henry", "Horrid Henry: Mega-Mean Time Machine", and
"Horrid Henry: Mummy's Curse" respectively.

This collection first published in Great Britain in 2021 by Hodder and Stoughton

1 3 5 7 9 10 8 6 4 2

ISBN 978 1 5101 0875 2

Printed and bound in Great Britain by Clays Ltd, Elcograf S.p.A.

The paper and board used in this book are from well-managed forests and
other responsible sources.

MIX
Paper from
responsible sources
FSC® C104740
www.fsc.org

Orion Children's Books
An imprint of
Hachette Children's Group
Part of Hodder and Stoughton
Carmelite House
50 Victoria Embankment
London EC4Y 0DZ

An Hachette UK Company
www.hachette.co.uk

www.hachettechildrens.co.uk
www.horridhenry.co.uk

CONTENTS

HORRID HENRY'S
OLYMPICS

CHOMP CHOMP CHOMP CHOMP

. . . **Burp**.

Ahhh! Horrid Henry scoffed the last crumb of Super Spicy Hedgehog crisps and burped again. So yummy. WOW. He'd eaten the entire pack in seventeen seconds. No one could guzzle crisps faster than **Horrid Henry**, especially when he was having to gobble them secretly in class. He'd never been caught, not even—

A dark, icy shadow fell across him.

"Are you eating in class, Henry?"

hissed **MISS BATTLE-AXE**.

"No," said Henry.

TEE HEE. Thanks to his *super-speedy* jaws, he'd already swallowed the evidence.

"Then where did this crisp packet come from?" said **MISS BATTLE-AXE**, pointing to the plastic bag on the floor.

Henry shrugged.

"Bert! Is this yours?"

"I dunno," said Beefy Bert.

"There is no eating in class," said Miss Battle-Axe. Why did she have to say the same things over and over? One day the Queen would

10

discover that she, *Boudicca Battle-Axe*, was her long-lost daughter and sweep her off to the palace, where

she would live a life of pampered luxury. But until then—

"Now, as I was saying, before I was so rudely interrupted," she **glared** at **Horrid Henry**, "our school will be having its very own Olympics. We'll be running and jumping and swimming and—"

"**Eating!**" yelled Horrid Henry.

"Quiet, Henry," snapped Miss Battle-Axe. "I want all of you to practise hard, both in school and out, to show—"

Horrid Henry stopped listening. It was so unfair. Wasn't it bad enough that every morning he had to *heave* his heavy bones out of bed to go to school, without wasting any of his precious **TV-WATCHING** time running and jumping and swimming? He was a *terrible* runner. He was a

pathetic jumper. He was a **hopeless** swimmer — though he did have his five-metre badge . . . Besides, Aerobic Al was sure to win every medal. In fact they should just give them all to him now and save everyone else a load of bother.

Shame, thought Horrid Henry, that the things he was so good at never got prizes. If there was a medal for who could watch TV the longest, or who could eat the most *sweets*, or who was *quickest* out of the classroom door when the home bell

rang, well, he'd be covered in gold
from head to toe.

"Go on, Susan! Jump higher."

"I'm jumping as high as I can," said
Sour Susan.

"That's not high," said MOODY
MARGARET. "A
tortoise could
jump higher
than you."

"Then get a tortoise," snapped Susan sourly.

"You're just a lazy lump."

"You're just a moody meanie."

"Lump."

"Meanie."

"**LUMP!**"

"**MEANIE!**"

SLAP!

SLAP!

"Whatcha doin'?" asked Horrid Henry, leaning over the garden wall.

"Go away, Henry," said Margaret.

"Yeah, Henry," said Susan.

"I can stand in my own garden if I want to," said Henry.

"Just ignore him," said Margaret.

"We're practising for the school Olympics," said Susan.

Horrid Henry snorted.

"I don't see you practising," said Margaret.

"That's 'cause I'm doing my own Olympics, *frog-face*," said Henry.

16

His jaw dropped.
YES! YES! A
thousand times yes!

Why hadn't he thought of
this before? Of course he should set
up his own Olympics. And have the
competitions he'd always wanted to
have. A name-calling competition!
A chocolate-eating competition! A
crisp-eating competition! A who-

could-watch-the-
most-TVs-at-
the-same-time
competition!

He'd make sure he had competitions that he could win. *The Henry Olympics.*

The Holympics. And the prizes would be . . . the prizes would be . . . masses and masses of CHOCOLATE!

"Can Ted and Gordon and I be in your Olympics?" said Perfect Peter.

"NO!" said Henry. Who'd want some nappy babies competing? They'd spoil everything, they'd—

Wait a minute . . .

"Of course you can, Peter," said Henry smoothly. "That will be one

pound each."

"Why?" said Ted.

"To pay for the **SUPER FANTASTIC PRIZES**, of course," said Henry. "Each champion will win a massive prize of . . . chocolate!"

Peter's face fell.

"Oh," he said.

"And a medal," added Henry quickly.

"Oh," said Peter, beaming.

"How **massive?**" said Margaret.

"Armfuls and armfuls," said Horrid

Henry. His mouth watered just thinking about it.

"Hmmm," said Margaret. "Well, I think there should be a *speed* haircutting competition. And dancing."

"Dancing?" said Henry. Well, why not? He was a brilliant dancer. His **elephant stomp** would win any competition hands down. "Okay."

Margaret and Susan plonked down one pound each.

"By the way, that's ballroom dancing," said Margaret.

"No way," said Henry.

"No ballroom dancing,
then we won't enter,"
said Margaret. "And
Linda and Gurinder
and Kate and
Fiona and Soraya
won't either."

Horrid Henry considered. He was
sure to win everything else, so why
not let her have a TINY victory? And
the more people who entered, the
more chocolate for him!

"Okay," said Henry.

"Bet you're scared I'll win everything," said Margaret.

"Am not."

"Are too."

"I can eat more sweets than you any day."

"Ha!" said Margaret. "I'd like to see you try."

"The Purple Hand Gang can beat the Secret Club and the Best Boys Club, no sweat," said Horrid Henry. "Bring it on."

THE REAL OLYMPICS ARE HERE!

TIRED OF BORING OLD SWIMMING AND RUNNING? OF COURSE YOU ARE!

NOW'S YOUR CHANCE TO COMPETE IN THE

HOLYMPICS

THE GREATEST OLYMPICS OF ALL!!!

SPEED-EATING SWEETS! TV WATCHING!

CRISP EATING! BURP TO THE BEAT!

BALLROOM DANCING. SPEED HAIRCUTTING.

ENTRY FEE £1 FOR THE CHANCE TO WIN LOADS OF CHOCOLATE!!!!!

"Hang on," said Margaret. "What's with calling this the *Holympics?* It should be the **MOLYMPICS**. I came up with the haircutting and dancing competitions."

"'Cause **MOLYMPICS** is a terrible name," said Henry.

"So's **HOLYMPICS**," said Margaret.

"Actually," said Peter, "I think it should be called the **Polympics**."

"Shut up, **worm**," said Henry.

"Yeah, worm," said Margaret.

"**MUM!**" screamed Henry.
"MUM!!!!!!!!"

Mum came running out of the shower.

"What is it, Henry?" she said, **dripping** water all over the floor. "Are you all right?"

"I need 𝓈𝓌𝑒𝑒𝓉𝓈," he said.

"You got me out of the shower because you need sweets?" she repeated.

"I need to practise for the sweet speed-eating competition," said Henry. "For my Olympics."

"Absolutely not," said Mum.

Horrid Henry was outraged.

"How am I supposed to win if I can't practise?" he howled. "You're always telling me to practise stuff. And now when I want to you won't let me."

Bookings for *Henry's Olympics* were brisk. Everyone in Henry's class —

and a few from Peter's — wanted
to compete. Horrid Henry gazed
happily at the 45 pounds' worth of
CHOCOLATE and crisps piled
high on his bed. **Wow. Wow. Mega
mega wow.** Boxes and boxes and
boxes filled with yummy, yummy
sweets! Giant bar after giant bar of
chocolate. His *HOLYMPICS* would have
the best prizes ever. And he, Henry,
fully expected to win most of them.
He'd win enough chocolate to last
him a lifetime AND have the glory of
coming first, for once.

27

Horrid Henry gazed at the chocolate prize mountain. The chocolate prize mountain gazed back at him, and winked.

Wait.

He, Henry, was doing ALL the work. Surely it was only fair if he got something for his valuable time. He should have kept a bit of money back to cover his expenses.

Horrid Henry removed a

GIANT CHOCOLATE BAR

from the pile.

After all, I do need to practise for the speed-eating contest, he thought, tearing off the wrapper and shoving a **massive** piece into his mouth. And then another. Oh boy, was that chocolate γummγ. In a few seconds, it was gone.

Yeah! **Horrid Henry**, chocolate-eating champion of the universe!

You know, thought Henry, gazing at the chocolate mound teetering precariously on his bed, I think I

bought too many prizes. And I do need
to practise for my event . . .

What a **GREAT DAY**, thought
Horrid Henry happily. He'd won
the sweet speed-eating competition
(though Greedy Graham had come a
close second), the crisp-eating contest
AND the name-calling one. (Peter had
run off screaming when Henry called
him **Wibble Wobble Pants, Nappy
Noodle** and **Odiferous**.)

Rude Ralph won "**Burp to the Beat**".

Margaret and
Susan won
best ballroom
dancers. Vain
Violet was
the surprise winner of the speed
haircutting competition. Weepy
William . . . well, his hair would grow
back — eventually.

Best of all, Aerobic Al didn't win
a thing.

The winners gathered round to
collect their prizes.

"Where's my chocolate, Henry?" said

MOODY MARGARET.

"And there had better be **loads** like you promised," said Vain Violet.

Horrid Henry reached into the big prize bag.

Now, where was the ballroom dancing prize? He pulled out a CHOCO BLOCO. Yikes, was that all the chocolate he had left? He rummaged around some more.

"A CHOCO BLOCO?" said Margaret slowly. "A single Choco Bloco?"

"They're very yummy," said Henry.

"And mine?" said Violet.

"And mine?" said Ralph.

"And mine for coming second?" said Graham.

"You're meant to share it!" screamed Horrid Henry, as he turned and ran.

Wow, thought Horrid Henry, as he fled down the road, Rude Ralph, Moody Margaret, Sour Susan, Vain Violet and Greedy Graham chasing after him, I'm pretty fast when I need to be. Maybe I should enter the school Olympics after all.

HORRID HENRY'S
CHICKEN

Oh joy! Oh rapture! It was the last day of school before the Easter break.

Henry had been counting down the weeks. Then the days. The hours. The minutes. No more school. No more **MISS BATTLE-AXE**. No more homework. Hello **TELLY**. Hello crisps. Hello pyjamas all day.

And hello *April Fool's Day* soon. Henry had great plans. Salt in the sugar bowl. Moving all the clocks forward. Mixing **shampoo** with GRASS and making Peter think FAT

FLUFFY had thrown up.

A few **pop-pop snapper-crackers** on the loo seat. Hanging Peter's underpants on his overhead light.

YIPPEE!

Nothing could spoil his happiness. Nothing. Nothing. Nothing. Not even if Mum insisted he play with Peter every single day. Not even if—

Squawk.

Squawk.

Squawk.

Horrid Henry scowled. And then he beamed. The holidays meant he wouldn't have to hear that horrible CHICKEN cackle for two whole weeks.

AAAAARRRGGHHH! Why couldn't his class have a rabbit, or a guinea pig, or a goldfish as a class pet? Instead, they had a CHICKEN. Not just any CHICKEN. A **HORRIBLE** CHICKEN. A **huge**, **HORRIBLE**, **EVIL** CHICKEN. Her name was Dolores. Ugh. Henry trembled just thinking about her mean chickeny eyes and her pointy chickeny feet and her fiery chickeny breath.

Horrid Henry was afraid of nothing (except injections). The **biggest** snake? Phooey. The **HAIRIEST** spider? Bah. But **Horrid Henry** was terrified of — shhhh — **CHICKENS.**

This was Henry's deepest, darkest secret. Who's scared of a **CHICKEN?** Who was so **CHICKEN** they were scared of a **CHICKEN?** Even Anxious Andrew happily fed Dolores.

But Horrid Henry was sure Dolores
was out to get him. Whenever he
walked past her coop she *glared*.
Henry had **NIGHTMARES** about
her chasing him with her jabbing,
stabbing, peck-peck-pecking beak.

EEEEEEK!

Henry shuddered and poked Ralph.

"I dare you to burp," whispered Henry.

"Stop burping, Ralph!" snapped **MISS BATTLE-AXE**.

"I have an important announcement," she added, fixing them with her Medusa glare. "Sad as I know you all are not to be in school for such a long time . . ."

As if, thought **Horrid Henry**.

"I'm happy to tell you that one lucky person will be having Dolores for the holidays."

"I want her," screamed **MOODY MARGARET**.

"I want her," screamed Inky Ian.

"I want her," drooled Greedy Graham.

"Ugg," grunted Stone-Age Steven.

"This wouldn't happen in Norway," said Norwegian Norris.

"**Silence!**" roared Miss Battle-Axe. "I've put all your names into a hat, and the winner gets Dolores."

Horrid Henry

picked up his pencil and
started drawing a monster dangling
MISS BATTLE-AXE from its acid-
dripping mouth all over his spelling
test. Phew. He was safe. He never
won anything. Who knew being
UNLUCKY would pay off one day?

Miss Battle-Axe reached into the
hat.

"And the lucky person having
Dolores is . . ." said Miss Battle-Axe,
peering at the slip of paper,
". . . Henry!"

"Wah," wailed Weepy William.

"What?" said Henry. He stopped drawing daggers. What was she telling him off for now?

"You've got Dolores," said Miss Battle-Axe.

He . . . what?

He had . . . Dolores? Deadly Dolores? The **FOULEST FOWL** on the planet? That **MONSTER** in feathers? That demented demon?

Horrid Henry opened his mouth to scream, NOOOOOO! I DON'T WANT HER!!!!!!!

Then he shut his mouth. What if someone suspected his **TERRIBLE** secret? That he, Horrid Henry, the **terror of teachers**, the squisher of sitters, the fearless leader of a pirate gang, was scared of — a **CHICKEN**. He'd never hear the end of the teasing and squawking.

Dolores *glared* at Henry.

Henry *glared* at Dolores.

Was it his imagination, or was she already sharpening her beak?

Henry gulped.

Actually, why was he worried?

His **MEAN**, **HORRIBLE** parents would never let him have a (HICKEN. He'd bring her home, and then Mum would make him take her straight back to school. Sorted.

"What fun, a (HICKEN," said Mum.

"**YUM**, **YUM**, think of all the *fresh eggs* we'll be having," said Dad.

"Henry, I expect you to take good care of her," said Mum. "That means cleaning out her box and letting her roam in the garden during the day as well as feeding her."

Horrid Henry could scarcely breathe. Was Mum **INSANE?** He could just about cope with throwing some corn at Dolores from a safe distance. But Mum wanted him to . . . to . . . **CLEAN UP CHICKEN POO?** Dolores would be lying in wait for him. His last moments on earth — covered in chicken poo while a marauding chicken ripped him limb from limb.

AAAARRRRGGGHHHH!

Horrid Henry avoided Deadly Dolores for as long as he could.

"No pocket money and no 📺 until you take care of that (HICKEN," said Dad.

"Later," said Henry. His heart was pounding.

"Right now," said Mum.

"No more excuses," said Dad.

"I always clean out FLUFFY'S litter box without being asked," said Perfect Peter.

"Then why don't you sleep in it, you **poopy pants worm**," said Henry.

"Mum," wailed Peter. "Henry called me a poopy pants worm."

"Stop being HORRID, Henry, and clean out that CHICKEN," said Mum.

"The eggs will go rotten if you don't collect them," said Dad.

"Eggs! Eggs! Eggs!" said Peter. "We want eggs."

Eggs?! Who cared about eggs?

While they were all fussing about eggs he'd be pecked to death by **Dracula Chicken**.

"OKAY," screamed Horrid Henry. Serve them right when they went looking for him and all that was left was a shoe and some bones.

Blood-sucking, cackling CHICKEN, muttered Henry. Bet she really did belong to **Dracula**. Bet her real name was **Cackula**.

Slowly, he walked towards the little red hen house at the end of the garden, carrying fresh straw, some

old newspaper and a rake. Ugh.
Bleccch. Gross. Clean out the hen
house? Clean out the hen house?! He,
Henry, have to touch . . . CHICKEN POO?
NOOOOOOOO!

Henry was sure **Cackula** did it on
purpose. Surely no normal CHICKEN
could make such a mess? She did
it to lure him closer. The moment
he touched her straw, he knew
she'd charge at him, wielding her

TERRIFYING beak and scratching claws. **Cackula** didn't eat corn and grubs. **Cackula** ate — Henrys!

Horrid Henry peeked in through the chicken wire. Maybe he could take her by surprise, he thought.

But no. There she was, lying in wait, her evil eyes glinting.

Horrid Henry trembled and stepped back.

Then he squared his shoulders. What was he, a **man** or a . . . a . . . CHICKEN?

CHICKEN, he squeaked.

I will not be defeated by a CHICKEN

named Dolores, he thought.

He opened the hen house door the TEENSIEST WEENSIEST bit.

Squawk!

Squawk!

Squawk!

A stinky, smelly blast hit him in the face as Deadly Dolores reared off her perch.

Henry slammed the hen house door shut. He stood there, gasping and

panting. Wow. What a lucky escape from **DEATH BY CHICKEN**.

He might not be so fortunate next time.

There was NO way he was going near that **murderous** beast.

But what to do, what to do? He could hardly admit he was — gulp — scared of a **CHICKEN**. And even if

by some **MIRACLE** he survived,
who wanted to spend their precious
holidays clearing up (HICKEN POO?

When he was *king*, all chickens
would be banned unless they were
wrapped in cellophane or coated in
breadcrumbs.

His holiday was ruined.

"Here, chick chick chick," cooed
a little voice behind him. "I've got a
lovely treat for you."

"PWOOAH PWOOAH PWOOAH," went Dolores,
pretending to be a sweet, friendly fowl.

"Peter's here, you lovely fluffy

little chicken," cheeped Peter. "Can I collect the eggs, Henry?"

"No," said Henry automatically.

"Please?"

"**NO!**"

"Why?" said Peter.

Suddenly Henry froze. What if . . . what if . . . what if he could get Peter to do his **DIRTY** work for him? That would be the best, the **GREATEST** trick ever in the history of the world. No, the universe!

Henry beckoned Peter closer and whispered in his ear.

"I can't let you because they're *magic* eggs. But if you tell anyone you'll be mashed to smithereens," said Henry.

"What do you mean, they're *magic* eggs?" said Peter.

"Keep your voice down," hissed Henry. "Just what I said. So no way are you going near my *magic* CHICKEN."

"How do you know she's magic?" said Peter.

"You've read *Jack and the Beanstalk,* haven't you?" said Henry. "Well,

Dolores is related to that CHICKEN. Except she lays *chocolate eggs*."

"Chocolate eggs?" said Peter. "How can she lay chocolate eggs?"

Henry shrugged. "How can she lay EGGIE EGGS? She's not the only magic CHICKEN in the world, you know. Where do you think all the chocolate eggs come from? But because I'm such a nice brother, I'll share the eggs with you."

"You will?" said Peter.

"But on one condition. You clean out the hen house, you get to keep the eggs."

"All the **chocolate eggs?**" said Peter. "Every single one?"

"Yup," said Henry.

"Okay," said Peter.

Tee hee, thought Henry. What a **worm** his brother was. Tricking him was so much fun. Really, he should do it more often.

Peter approached the hen box and reached inside. Henry, naturally, had an answer ready for when Peter found it empty.

"Duh, of course there aren't any magic eggs yet," he'd say. "You have to clean out her nest first. She's not going to lay a **chocolate egg** in a **POo HoUSE**, is she?"

That way, he'd get Peter to muck out the hen house for the entire holiday, hoping to get *magic* eggs. Ha! Sorted. He was a genius. His plan was *perfect*. No more **POo**. No more Dolores. **TV** here I come, thought Horrid Henry.

Perfect Peter squealed.

"Look what I've found," said Peter. He held out his hand. "There's **LOADS** and **LOADS** and **LOADS** of them."

Perfect Peter was holding a **chocolate egg**.

Huh?

What?

How could this be? Could there really be . . .

Horrid Henry forgot he was scared of (HICKENS.

Horrid Henry forgot **Cackula** was out to get him.

Horrid Henry shoved Peter aside and pushed the squawking Dolores off her nest.

There in the straw was a huge,

glistening pile of gleaming **chocolate eggs**.

"Come get us, Henry," cooed the eggs.

"Out of my way, **Worm**!" shrieked Henry.

"But you said—" shrieked Peter.

"That was then," screamed Henry, shoving Peter out of the way. "They're all mine."

"**MINE!**" screamed Peter.

"**MINE!**" screamed Henry.

"Gimme those eggs or the giant will get you," said Henry.

"What giant?" said Peter.

"I told you. Dolores belongs to the giant in *Jack and the Beanstalk*. He'll be coming for her . . . and then for **YOU!**"

"I don't think so," said Peter. He backed away, holding onto his egg. "And do you know why?"

"**NO**," snarled Horrid Henry, blocking Peter and snatching *chocolate eggs* from the nest as fast as he could. He felt like dancing for joy. He had a *magic* CHICKEN. He'd find a way to keep Dolores. He'd

tell **MISS BATTLE-AXE** they'd eaten her for Sunday lunch by mistake. Then he'd have chocolate forever. **Horrid Henry** hugged himself. He could set up a shop – **HENRY'S AMAZING CHOCOLATE EGGS**. People would come for miles to buy his chocolate and peek at his magic, *chocolate-egg*-laying CHICKEN. He'd charge them £100 just to look at Dolores.

He'd be rich, rich, rich!

"**APRIL FOOL!**" shouted Peter.

"**APRIL FOOL!**" shouted Mum.

"April Fool!" shouted Dad.

"Squawk!" cackled Dolores, ruffling her feathers.

Oh. Oh no. **Horrid Henry** had been so anxious about Dolores he'd completely forgotten about *April Fool's Day*.

"We thought you'd

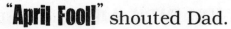

NEVER find them," said Mum.

"What took you so long?" said Dad.

"I tricked you, Henry," said Perfect Peter. He couldn't believe it. For once, he'd played a trick.

Horrid Henry stood still. His mind whirred.

But Horrid Henry was not the **FEARLESS LEADER OF A PIRATE GANG** for nothing.

"In your dreams, *Worm*," said Horrid Henry, stuffing a chocolate egg in his mouth. "I was just pretending to believe you."

He patted Dolores on the head. She wasn't *magic*, but she wasn't a **MONSTER**. Why on earth had he ever been **SCARED** of her?

He'd deal with Peter later. No one tried to trick **Horrid Henry** and lived to tell the tale.

Screams came from Peter's bedroom. Henry threw down his comic and ran to see.

There was Peter, covered in **gooey**

raw egg and holding a chocolate-
covered shell. GOOP dribbled down
his chin and shirt and splattered
onto his shoes.

"AAAARRRGGHHH!" squealed
Peter.

"April Fool!" shrieked
Horrid Henry.

HORRID
HENRY
UP, UP AND AWAY

oh wow! **Oh wow! oh boy oh boy oh boy!**

Horrid Henry could scarcely believe it. After years of him BEGGING and pleading and pleading and BEGGING, Horrid Henry's mean, **HORRIBLE** parents were finally taking him on an *aeroplane*. It was a dream come true.

Mum and Dad's idea of a great holiday was staying at home and weeding the garden. Or **WORSE**, forcing **HIM** to help weed the garden. Or **EVEN WORSE**, camping in a SMELLY

mosquito-filled swamp without TV or computers or **ANYTHING**.

GAG. **BLECCCCCCCCCH**.

YUCK.

These weren't holidays.

These were organised **CRUELTY** to children. One happy day, when Henry was **KING**, he'd make sure that kids decided where to go on holiday, and any parent who so much as *whispered* the words **GARDEN** or **CAMPING** or **FRESH AIR** would get **trampled** by stampeding penguins.

But now, at last, they were flying
off on a real vacation, to stay in a
hotel with twelve **HUGE** pools, wave
machines and room service and
EVERYTHING. It was like taking a
holiday in *heaven*.

Horrid Henry had never flown
on an aeroplane. But he knew all
about it. Stuck-up Steve had bragged
about the flight he and Rich Aunt
Ruby had just taken. Your own cabin
complete with baskets filled with
chocolates and **CRISPS**. *Luxury* beds.

Flight stewards at your beck and call
whenever you wanted more sweets
or an extra burger — OR THREE.
Non-stop **ice cream** and FIZZYWIZZ
drinks and TV and games. Any food
you liked, brought to you with a
SNAP of your fingers as you reclined
in your fabulous **comfy** chair.
Horrid Henry couldn't wait to be
soaring through the air, watching
every episode of *Terminator Gladiator*
or *Skeleton Skunk*, a **huge** bowl of
chocolates by his side. Best of all, his
parents couldn't nag him to do his

chores, finish his homework or turn off the TV. Not on a plane. He'd be *FREE*.

In fact, maybe he could fly the plane. How hard could it be? He could ride a bike. Maybe he could do a few *loop the loops* while he was *SOARING* through the clouds. **Pilot Henry**. With an **EJECTOR SEAT** for his younger brother, Perfect Peter.

But would the flight be long enough to play **EVERY** game and watch **EVERY** episode? Henry hoped so. He couldn't wait to relax in his own *mini-palace* in the sky.

The only bad thing was that for some reason his

NAPPY NOODLE

wormy worm

wibble wobble

POOPY PANTS

POOPSICLE

brother was coming too, instead of being put out with the recycling.

Horrid Henry **SCOWLED**. He couldn't wait to **SLAM** the door shut on his private cabin so he wouldn't have to see the **TOADY TOAD** for the whole flight.

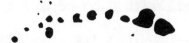

At last the great day arrived. After *checking* they had tickets and passports, and then *double-checking* they had tickets and passports, and then *triple-checking* they had tickets and passports, Henry, Peter, Mum and Dad finally arrived at the airport.

"**Out of ny way, worns!**" shrieked **Horrid Henry**, *ZOOMING* to the departure gate on his Marvin the Maniac Glidy-Glidy wheeled suitcase, **CRASHING** into people and **KNOCKING** over duty-free displays. "I've got a plane to catch."

"Don't be **HORRID**, Henry!" shouted Mum.

"HENRY, GET BACK HERE!" shouted Dad.

But **Horrid Henry** ignored them. Why queue when paradise beckoned? He'd already wasted **so** much time **WAITING** in line to check in, **WAITING** in line for security, **WAITING** in line to **WAIT** in line. Horrid Henry couldn't **WAIT** another **second**.

He ran ahead and jumped on to the jet, **pushing** and **SHOVING** past everyone waiting to board. He had to

make sure he got a window seat.
He dashed through the plane door
and stared. **OOH! Yes! Oh wow!**
Stuck-up Steve had been telling
the truth.

There were the **HUGE** reclining seats,
with the **MASSIVE** TVs and
fluffy pillows.

And, even better, there were plenty
which were still empty. Henry raced
to bag one by the window.

Horrid Henry sank into the
leather chair. It was **MASSIVE**.
There was the basket filled with

chocolates and **CRISPS**. The bell to
call the flight attendant. Or should
he say, his own personal butler.

And best of all, a
GINORMOUS TV screen
all for him. Just look at all the
channels on the remote control.
Horrid Henry's thumbs *itched*
to get started.

It was even better than he'd hoped.

But for some reason Horrid Henry's
parents didn't rush to bag their own
mini-palace. Instead, they stood in the
aisle with Peter, **GLARING** at him.

"Hurry up," said Henry. "Or you won't get a seat."

"Henry," said Dad. "We're not sitting here."

"Yeah, Henry," said Peter.

WHAT? Were they CRAZY? Was there somewhere even better? Maybe with a **swimming pool** and a *ski slope?*

"This is first class," said Mum.

"So?" said Henry, scooping up a fistful of sweets.

A flight attendant walked towards them, smiling.

"Hello! Welcome on board. I'm Greg, here to

make your flight a great one."

Then Greg caught sight of
Henry's ticket. His smile vanished.
He grabbed the sweets out of
Henry's hand.

"**Oi**," said Horrid Henry.
"GIVE THOSE BACK."

"Move," said Grumpy
Greg. **"AND MAKE IT
SNAPPY."**

"But I like it here," said Henry.
He held on to the plush armrests.

"Get up **NOW** or there will be **NO TV** during the flight," *hissed* Mum.

Reluctantly, Henry got out of his **KING-SIZE** seat.

Where they were going had better be good, he thought, **SCOWLING**, as he followed his parents down the aisle and through the curtain.

A gruesome sight met his eyes.

"**STOP!** Let's go back," protested Henry.

Henry's parents ignored him

and carried on walking.

DOWN, DOWN, DOWN they trudged,
towards the back of the plane.

The seats got **smaller** and
smaller and smaller. The aisles got
NARROWER and NARROWER and NARROWER.
Henry looked in horror at the
cramped rows.

"TURN BACK. TURN BACK. WHY ARE
WE GOING HERE?" he shouted.

Mum, Dad and Peter ignored him,
and continued SQUEEZING down the tiny
aisle to the second to last row of
seats in the middle by the TOILETS.

"Here," said Dad.

"This is nice and cosy," said Peter.

Horrid Henry was so shocked he couldn't move. Was this some **CRUEL** joke? Had he been *zapped* into the **ZOMBIE** dimension? These postage stamp seats weren't even by a window.

"**I CAN'T SIT HERE!**" screamed Horrid Henry. "I'll suffocate."

"Sit down," ordered Grumpy Greg. He clicked his fingers. "And make it **SNAPPY**. You're blocking the aisle."

Reluctantly, Horrid Henry **HEAVED** himself into his teeny tiny **lumpy**

bumpy seat.

Dad **SQUEEZED** into his tiny seat.

Mum **SQUEEZED** into her tiny seat.

Peter **SQUEEZED** into his tiny seat.

"The holiday starts here," said Dad cheerfully. "Buckle up."

Across the aisle a red-faced baby
began to howl.

"*WAAAAAAAHHHH!*"
And another.

"*WAAAAAAAAHHHH.*"
And another.

"*WAAAAAAAAHHHHH.*"
Then Horrid Henry saw a
terrible sight.

"**WHERE'S MY TV?**" he wailed,
kicking and hurling
himself
backwards in
the seat.

"**OWWWWW**," yelped the man sitting in front of him.

"**OWWWWW**," yelped the woman sitting behind him.

"**WHERE'S MY TV?**" bellowed Henry again.

"I guess they don't have them back here," said Mum.

"You can read a book," said Dad.

"I've brought loads of books," said Peter. "You can borrow some of mine. I've got THE HAPPY NAPPY, BUNNY'S BEST HOLIDAY, KITTEN'S MITTEN—"

"**NO!**" howled Henry. "I want to

watch TV. I want to play games."

Horrid Henry

kicked the seat as
hard as he could,
then *FLUNG*
himself backwards
as **FEROCIOUSLY**
as he could.

"AAAARRRGGGHH,"

yelped the man in front again.
He stood up. Orange juice
dripped down his shirt. "You
made me spill my drink.
I'm soaked."

"**AAAARRRGGGHH**," yelped the woman behind him. She stood up. Coffee **dripped** down her jumper. "You made me spill my drink too."

Too late, **Horrid Henry** remembered an extra bit of Steve's bragging.

"Of course YOU'LL be flying economy," Stuck-up Steve had said.

"No I won't." Horrid Henry hadn't known what economy was. But now, unfortunately, he did.

The plane took off. The babies howled. Henry **kicked**.

"**ARRRRRRGGGH**," yelled the man in front. He stood up. Tomato juice **DRIBBLED** down his face onto his shirt. "Stop **kicking** me!"

"Don't be **horrid**, Henry!" shouted Mum.

Mum read her book.

Dad read his book.

Peter read his book.

Horrid Henry **kicked**
the seat in front.

"**Beef burger**,
chicken, or VEGETABLE
BAKE WITH SPROUTS?" asked
Chirpy Cheryl, making her way
slowly down the aisle with her trolley.

"**Beef burger**? *Chicken*?
VEGETABLE BAKE?"

Henry's tummy RUMBLED.

At least there were **burgers**.

"I want a **burger**," said Henry, when Cheryl eventually reached their row.

"We've only got VEGETABLE BAKE WITH SPROUTS left," said Chirpy Cheryl.

"Oh yum," said Perfect Peter, as green sludge was SLOPPED onto his tray table.

"What happened to the **burgers**?" wailed Horrid Henry.

"Gone," said Chirpy Cheryl.

GONE?

Was there no end to the misery he was enduring?

No TV. No burger.

Squished into a seat that would crush a grasshopper.

A huge queue for the *smelly* toilets.

Screaming babies.

Horrid Henry kicked the seat as hard as he could.

"AAARRRGGHH!" yelped the man in front. He stood up. Vegetable bake dripped down his hair on to his clothes.

97

SNORE SNORE.

SNORE SNORE.

Mum was SNORING.

Dad was SNORING.

Perfect Peter was SNORING.

Horrid Henry was **STARVING**.

KICK KICK
KICK
THUNK THUNK
THUNK

"**ARRRRRRGGGH!**" yelped the man in front. "**MY TEA!**"

"**ARRRRRRGGGH!**" yelped the woman behind. "**MY COFFEE!**"

"*Wah!*" a baby wailed.

Another joined in.

"*Wah!*"

And another.

"*WAAAAHHHH!*"

Horrid Henry could stand it no longer. He'd go mad if he stayed in this **HELLHOLE**. Unless he starved to death first. When Mum and Dad woke up, they'd find a shrivelled bag

of bones in his seat. Then they'd be
sorry. But it would be too late.

Goodbye, cruel world, thought
Henry.

And then Horrid Henry had a
brilliant, SPECTACULAR idea.
Why hadn't he thought of it before?
He didn't have to put up with this
torture. He didn't have to starve
or shrivel into a mummy.

Horrid Henry checked up
the aisle.

Horrid Henry checked down
the aisle.

The coast was clear.

He **SQUEEZED** past snoring Mum.
Then *quick* as he could, he ran up
to the front and slipped under the
curtain and into first class.

There were loads of empty seats
waiting for him.

Horrid Henry nabbed one by the
window. He stretched out his
aching legs and **GRABBED** the remote.
Then he **SNATCHED** a bar of
chocolate and stuffed it in his mouth.

Ahh. This was where he belonged.
The lap of luxury. Peace at last.

A **DARK SHADOW** fell over him.

"**OI!** That's not your seat. Get back where you belong and **MAKE IT SNAPPY**," snapped Grumpy Greg.

"**NO!**" shrieked Horrid Henry. "**NOOOOOOO!**" They'd have to drag him away.

A long-haired man, dozing under a hat across the aisle, looked up. He stared at Henry.

"So sorry to disturb you, sir," said Grumpy Greg. "He'll be removed **immediately**."

"Henry? Is that you?" asked the

long-haired man.

It was **KING KILLER**, lead singer of the **KILLER BOY RATS**, Henry's favourite band. Henry had met him backstage when **KING KILLER** had invited Henry to be his guest at the **MANIC PANIC** concert.

"**KING!**" said Horrid Henry.

"Great to see you, Henry," said
KING KILLER.

"Get back to your seat," ordered
Grumpy Greg. "And make it **SNAPPY**."

"It's OK," said **KING KILLER**. "He's
with the band."

"Gonna be a rock star . . . and
you ain't!" **Horrid Henry** hummed
his favourite Killer Boy Rats song as
he popped another *chocolate* into his
mouth. Decisions, decisions. Another

burger, or more *cake*? Another episode of *Terminator Gladiator*, or should he change channels to *Marvin the Maniac*? More **CRISPS**? More *ice cream*?

"Oh steward," said Horrid Henry, "bring me some more chocolate cake and . . . make it snappy!"

HORRID HENRY'S
HOLIDAY

Horrid Henry hated holidays.

Henry's idea of a SUPER holiday was sitting on the sofa eating crisps and watching TV.

Unfortunately, his parents usually had other plans.

Once they took him to see some castles. But there were no castles.

There were only piles of stones and broken walls.

"Never again," said Henry.

The next year he had to go to a lot of museums.

"Never again," said Mum and Dad.

Last year they went to the seaside.

"The sun is too **HOT**," Henry whined.

"The water is too cold,"
Henry whinged.

"The food is γυcκγ," Henry grumbled.

"The bed is **lumpy**," Henry moaned.

This year they decided to try something different.

"We're going camping in France," said Henry's parents.

"**HOORAY!**" said Henry.

"You're happy, Henry?" said Mum. Henry had never been happy about any holiday plans before.

"Oh yes," said Henry. Finally, finally, they were doing something good.

Henry knew all about camping from Moody Margaret. Margaret had been camping with her family.

They had stayed in a big tent with *comfy beds*, a *fridge*, a *cooker*, a *loo*, a *shower*, a *heated swimming pool*, a *disco*, and a *great big giant TV with seven channels*.

"Oh boy!" said Horrid Henry.

"*Bonjour!*" said Perfect Peter.

The great day arrived at last.
Horrid Henry, Perfect Peter, Mum and
Dad boarded the ferry for France.

Henry and Peter had never been
on a boat before.

Henry jumped on and off the seats.

Peter did a lovely drawing.

The boat went UP and DOWN
and UP and DOWN.

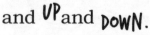

Henry ran back and forth between the aisles.

Peter pasted stickers in his notebook.

The boat went UP and DOWN and UP and DOWN.

Henry sat on a revolving chair and spun round.

Peter played with his puppets.

The boat went UP and DOWN and UP and DOWN.

Then Henry and Peter ate a big greasy lunch of sausages and chips in the café.

The boat went

UP and DOWN, and UP and DOWN, and UP and DOWN.

Henry began to feel queasy.

Peter began to feel queasy.

Henry's face went green.

Peter's face went green.

"I think I'm going to be SICK," said Henry, and threw up all over Mum.

"I think I'm going to be—" said Peter, and threw up all over Dad.

"Oh no," said Mum.

"Never mind," said Dad. "I just know this will be our best holiday ever."

Finally, the boat arrived in France.

After driving and driving and driving they reached the campsite.

It was even better than Henry's dreams. The tents were as big as houses. Henry heard the happy sound of TVs blaring, music

playing, and children splashing and shrieking. The sun shone. The sky was blue.

"**WOW**, this looks great," said Henry.

But the car drove on.

"**STOP!**" said Henry. "You've gone too far."

"We're not staying in that **AWFUL** place," said Dad.

They drove on.

"Here's our campsite," said Dad. "A *real* campsite!"

Henry stared at the bare rocky ground under the *cloudy* grey sky.

There were three small tents flapping in the wind. There was a single tap. There were a few trees. There was **NOTHING ELSE**.

"It's wonderful!" said Mum.

"It's wonderful!" said Peter.

"But where's the TV?" said Henry.

"No TV here, thank goodness," said Mum. "We've got books."

"But where are the **beds?**"
said Henry.

"No beds here, thank goodness,"
said Dad. "We've got sleeping bags."

"But where's the pool?" said Henry.

"No pool," said Dad. "We'll swim
in the river."

"Where's the toilet?" said Peter.

Dad pointed at a distant cubicle.
Three people stood waiting "All the
way over there?" said Peter. "I'm not
complaining," he added quickly.

Mum and Dad unpacked the car.
Henry stood and scowled.

"Who wants to help put up the tent?"
asked Mum.

"I do!" said Dad.

"I do!" said Peter.

Henry was horrified. "WE HAVE TO PUT UP OUR OWN TENT?"

"Of course," said Mum.

"I don't like it here," said Henry. "I want to go camping in the other place."

"That's not camping," said Dad. "Those tents have *beds* in them. And *loos*. And *showers*. And *fridges*. And *cookers*, and *TVs*. **Horrible**." Dad shuddered.

"Horrible," said Peter.

"And we have such a **lovely snug** tent here," said Mum. "Nothing modern — just wooden pegs and poles."

"Well, I want to stay there," said Henry.

"We're staying here," said Dad.

"**NO!**" screamed Henry.

"**YES!**" screamed Dad.

I am sorry to say that Henry then had the *LONGEST*, **LOUDEST**, noisiest, shrillest, most **HORRIBLE** tantrum you can imagine.

Did you think that a **horrid** boy like Henry would like nothing better than sleeping on hard

rocky ground
in a soggy sleeping
bag without a
pillow?

You thought
wrong.

Henry liked
comfy beds.

Henry liked CRISP SHEETS.

Henry liked hot baths.

Henry liked *microwave dinners*,
TV, and NOISE.

He did not like cold showers, *fresh air*,
and quiet.

Far off in the distance the sweet
sound of loud music drifted
towards them.

"Aren't you glad we're not staying
in that **AWFUL** noisy place?" said Dad.

"Oh yes," said Mum.

"Oh yes," said Perfect Peter.

Henry pretended he was a
bulldozer come to knock down tents
and squash campers.

"Henry, don't barge the tent!"
yelled Dad.

Henry pretended he was a hungry
Tyrannosaurus Rex.

"**OW!**" shrieked Peter.

"**Henry, don't be horrid!**"
yelled Mum.

She looked up at the dark *cloudy* sky.

"It's going to rain," said Mum.

"Don't worry," said Dad. "It
never rains when I'm camping."

"The boys and I will go and collect
some more firewood," said Mum.

"I'm not moving," said
Horrid Henry.

While Dad made a campfire,
Henry played his boom-box
as loud as he could,

stomping in time to the terrible
music of the Killer Boy Rats.

"Henry, turn that noise down this
minute," said Dad.

Henry pretended not to hear.

"**HENRY!**" yelled Dad.

"*TURN
THAT
DOWN!*"

Henry turned
the volume down
the teeniest
tiniest fraction.

The **TERRIBLE** sounds of the Killer Boy Rats continued to **BOOM** over the quiet campsite.

Campers emerged from their tents and shook their fists. Dad switched off Henry's tape player.

"Anything wrong, Dad?" asked Henry, in his sweetest voice.

"No," said Dad.

Mum and Peter returned carrying armfuls of firewood.

It started to *drizzle*.

"This is fun," said Mum, slapping a mosquito.

"Isn't it?" said Dad. He was heating up some tins of baked beans.

The *drizzle* turned into a **DOWNPOUR**.

The *wind* blew. The campfire hissed, and went out.

"Never mind," said Dad brightly. "We'll eat our baked beans cold."

Mum was *snoring*.

Dad was *snoring*.

Peter was *snoring*.

Henry tossed and turned. But whichever way he turned in his damp sleeping bag, he seemed to be lying on sharp, pointy stones.

Above him, mosquitoes whined.

I'll never get to sleep, he thought, kicking Peter.

How am I going to bear this for fourteen days?

Around four o'clock on Day Five the family huddled inside the **COLD, DAMP, SMELLY** tent listening to the howling wind and the pouring rain.

"Time for a walk!" said Dad.

"**Great idea!**" said Mum, sneezing. "I'll get the boots."

"**Great idea!**" said Peter, sneezing. "I'll get the macs."

"But it's pouring outside," said Henry.

"So?" said Dad. "What better time to go for a walk?"

"I'm not coming," said Horrid Henry.

"I am," said Perfect Peter. "I don't mind the rain."

Dad poked his head outside the tent.

"The rain has stopped," he said.
"I'll remake the fire.

"I'm not coming," said Henry.

"We need more firewood," said
Dad. "Henry can stay here and collect
some. And make sure it's dry."

Henry poked his head outside the
tent. The rain had stopped, but the
sky was still cloudy. The fire spat.

I won't go, thought Henry. The
forest will be all MUDDY and wet.

He looked round to see if there was
any wood closer to home.

That was when he saw the thick,

dry wooden pegs holding up all the
tents.

Henry looked to the left.

Henry looked to the right.

No one was around.

If I just take a few pegs from each
tent, he thought, they'll never be
missed.

When Mum and Dad came back
they were delighted.

"What a lovely roaring fire," said Mum.

"Clever you to find some dry
wood," said Dad.

The wind blew.

Henry dreamed he was **floating** in
a cold river.

Floating, *floating*, *floating*.

He woke up. He shook his head.

He **was floating**. The tent was filled
with cold muddy water.

Then the tent **collapsed** on top of them.

Henry, Peter, Mum and Dad stood outside in the rain and stared at the river of water gushing through their collapsed tent.

All round them soaking wet campers were staring at their collapsed tents.

Peter Sneezed.

Mum Sneezed.

Dad Sneezed.

Henry **coughed**, (CHOKED,

SPLUTTERED and **SNEEZED**.

"I don't understand it," said Dad.

"This tent *never* collapses."

"What are we going to do?" said Mum.

"I know," said Henry. "I've got a very good idea."

Two hours later Mum, Dad, Henry and Peter were sitting on a sofa-bed inside a tent as big as a house, eating CRISPS and watching TV.

The sun was shining. The sky was blue.

"Now this is what I call a holiday!" said Henry.

HORRID HENRY'S

HIKE

Horrid Henry looked out of the window. AAARRRGGGHHH! It was a lovely day. The sun was shining. The birds were tweeting. The breeze was blowing. Little fluffy clouds floated by in a bright blue sky.

RATS.

Why couldn't it be RAINING? Or hailing? Or sleeting?

Any minute, any second, it would happen . . . the words he'd been dreading, the words he'd give anything not to hear, the words —

"Henry! Peter! Time to go for a **WALK**," called Mum.

"Yippee!" said Perfect Peter. "I can wear my new yellow wellies!"

"**NO!**" screamed Horrid Henry.

Go for a walk! Go for a walk! Didn't he walk enough already? He walked to school. He walked home from school. He walked to the TV. He walked to the computer. He walked to the sweet jar and all the way back to the comfy black chair. **Horrid Henry** walked plenty. **Ugghh**. The last thing he needed was more walking. More

chocolate, yes. More **CRISPS**, yes. More *walking*? No way! Why oh why couldn't his parents ever say, "Henry! Time to play on the computer." Or "Henry, **STOP** doing your homework this minute! Time to turn on the **TV**."

But no. For some reason his **mean**, **HORRIBLE** parents thought he spent too much time sitting indoors. They'd

been threatening for weeks to make him go on a family walk. Now the DREADFUL moment had come. His precious weekend was ruined.

Horrid Henry HATED nature. Horrid Henry HATED fresh air. What could be more boring than walking up and down streets staring at lamp posts? Or sloshing across some stupid MUDDY park? Nature smelled. UGGH! He'd much rather be inside watching TV.

Mum stomped into the sitting room.

"Henry! Didn't you hear me calling?"

"No," lied Henry.

"Get your wellies on, we're going," said Dad, rubbing his hands. "What a *lovely* day."

"I don't want to go for a walk," said Henry. "I want to watch **Rapper Zapper** Zaps **Terminator Gladiator**."

"But Henry," said Perfect Peter, "*fresh air* and *exercise* are so good for you."

"**I don't care!**" shrieked Henry.

Horrid Henry stomped downstairs and *flung* open the front door. He breathed in deeply, **HOPPED** on one foot, then shut the door.

147

"There! Done it. Fresh air and exercise," snarled Henry.

"Henry, we're going," said Mum. "Get in the car."

Henry's ears pricked up.

"The car?" said Henry. "I thought we were going for a walk."

"We are," said Mum. "In the countryside."

"Hurray!" said Perfect Peter. "A nice long walk."

"NOOOO!" howled Henry. Plodding along in the boring old park was bad enough, with its mouldy leaves

and **DOG POO** and stumpy trees. But at least the park wasn't very big. But the countryside?

The countryside was **enormous!** They'd be walking for hours, days, weeks, months, till his legs wore down to stumps and his feet **fell off**. And the countryside was so **dangerous!** Horrid Henry was sure he'd be **swallowed** up by quicksand or **TRAMPLED** to death by marauding chickens.

"I live in the city!" shrieked Henry.
"I don't want to go to the country!"

"Time you got out more," said Dad.

"But look at those clouds," moaned
Henry, pointing to a 𝒻𝓁𝓊𝒻𝒻𝓎 wisp.
"We'll get **soaked**."

"A little water never hurt anyone,"
said Mum.

Oh yeah? Wouldn't they be sorry
when he died of PNEUMONIA.

"I'M STAYING HERE AND THAT'S FINAL!"
screamed Henry.

"Henry, we're waiting," said Mum.

"Good," said Henry.

"I'm all ready, Mum," said Peter.

"I'm going to start deducting pocket money," said Dad. "5p, 10p, 15p, 20—"

Horrid Henry pulled on his wellies, stomped out of the door and got in the car. He **SLAMMED** the door as hard as he could. It was so unfair! Why did he never get to do what he wanted to do? Now he would miss the first time **Rapper Zapper** had ever slugged it out with **Terminator Gladiator**. And all because he had to go on a long, boring, exhausting, **HORRIBLE** hike. He was so miserable he didn't even have the energy to kick Peter.

"Can't we just walk round the block?" moaned Henry.

"N-O spells no," said Dad. "We're going for a lovely walk in the countryside and that's that."

Horrid Henry **slumped** miserably in his seat. Boy would they be sorry when he was **gobbled** up by goats. **Boo Hoo**, if only we hadn't gone on that walk in the wilds, Mum would wail.

Henry was right, we should have listened to him, Dad would **SOB**. I miss Henry, Peter would **howl**. I'll never eat goat's cheese again. And now it's too late, they would **SHRIEK**.

If only, thought Horrid Henry. That would serve them right.

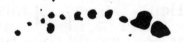

All too soon, Mum pulled into a car park on the edge of a small wood.

"**Wow**," said Perfect Peter. "Look at all those **lovely** trees."

"Bet there are **WEREWOLVES** hiding

there," muttered Henry. "And I hope they come and eat you!"

"Mum!" squealed Peter. "Henry's trying to scare me."

"Don't be **horrid**, Henry," said Mum.

Horrid Henry looked around him. There was a gate, leading to endless meadows bordered by hedgerows. A **MUDDY** path wound through the trees and across the fields. A church spire stuck up in the distance.

"Right, I've seen the countryside, let's go home," said Henry.

Mum *glared* at him.

"What?" said Henry, scowling.

"Let's enjoy this *lovely* day," said Dad, sighing.

"So what do we do now?" said Henry.

"*Walk*," said Dad.

"Where?" said Henry.

"Just *walk*," said Mum, "and enjoy the *beautiful* scenery."

Henry groaned.

"We're heading for the lake," said Dad, striding off. "I've brought bread

and we can feed the
ducks."

"But **Rapper
Zapper** starts in an hour!"

"**TOUGH**," said Mum.

Mum, Dad and Peter headed through
the gate into the field. Horrid Henry
trailed behind them, walking as slowly
as he could.

"Ahh, breathe the *lovely* fresh air,"
said Mum.

"We should do this more often,"
said Dad.

Henry sniffed.

The **HORRIBLE** smell of manure filled his nostrils.

"Ewww, smelly," said Henry. "Peter, couldn't you wait?"

"MUM!" shrieked Peter. "Henry called me smelly."

"Did not!"

"Did too!"

"Did not, smelly."

"WAAAAAAAAA!" wailed Peter. "Tell him to stop!"

"Don't be **horrid**, Henry!" screamed Mum.

Her voice echoed. A dog walker passed her, and *glared*.

"Peter, would you rather run a mile, jump a stile, or eat a country *pancake*?" said Henry *sweetly*.

"Ooh," said Peter. "I love *pancakes*. And a country one must be even more delicious than a city one."

"HA HA," cackled Horrid Henry, sticking out his tongue. "Fooled you. Peter wants to eat COWPATS!"

"MUM!' screamed Peter.

Henry walked.

And walked.

And walked.

His legs felt **HEAVIER**, and **HEAVIER**, and **HEAVIER**.

"This field is muddy," **MOANED** Henry.

"I'm bored," **groaned** Henry.

"My feet hurt," **WHINED** Henry.

"Can't we go home? We've already walked miles," **WHINGED** Henry.

"We've been walking for ten minutes," said Dad.

"Please can we go on walks more

159

often?" said Perfect Peter. "Oh, look at those *fluffy little sheepies!*"

Horrid Henry **pounced**. He was a **zombie** biting the head off the hapless human.

"AAAAEEEEEE!" squealed Peter.

"**Henry!**" screamed Mum.

"Stop it!" screamed Dad. "Or no TV for a week."

When he was king, thought Horrid Henry, any parent who made their children go on a hike would be **DUMPED** barefoot in a *scorpion-infested* desert.

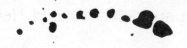

Plod.
Plod.
Plod.

Horrid Henry *dragged* his feet.
Maybe his **horrible MEAN** parents
would get fed up waiting for him and
turn back, he thought, kicking some
mouldy leaves.

Squelch.
Squelch.
Squelch.

Oh no, not another **MUDDY** meadow.
And then suddenly Horrid Henry

had an idea. What was he thinking? All that 𝒻𝓇ℯ𝓈𝒽 𝒶𝒾𝓇 must be rotting his brain. The sooner they got to the stupid lake, the sooner they could get home for the **Rapper Zapper** Zaps **Terminator Gladiator**.

"Come on, everyone, let's run!" shrieked Henry. "Race you down the hill to the lake!"

"That's the spirit, Henry," said Dad.

Horrid Henry dashed past Dad.

"**OW!**" shrieked Dad, tumbling into the 𝓈𝓉𝒾𝓃𝑔𝒾𝓃ℊ nettles.

Horrid Henry **whizzed** past Mum.

"EWW!" shrieked Mum, slipping in a cowpat.

SPLAT!

Horrid Henry **pushed** past Peter.

"Waaa!" wailed Peter. "My wellies are getting dirty."

Horrid Henry scampered down the **MUDDY** path.

"Wait, Henry!" yelped Mum. "It's too slipp— **AAAiiiEEEEE!**"

Mum slid down the path on her bottom.

"Slow down!" puffed Dad.

"I can't run that fast," wailed Peter.

But **Horrid Henry** raced on.

"Shortcut across the field!" he called. "Come on, slowcoaches!" The black and white cow grazing alone in the

middle raised its head.

"**HENRY!**" shouted Dad.

Horrid Henry kept running.

"I don't think that's a cow!" shouted
Mum.

The cow lowered its head and charged.

"**It's a bull!**" yelped Mum and Dad.

"**RUN!**"

"I said it was **dangerous** in the countryside!" gasped Henry, as everyone clambered over the stile in the nick of time. "Look, there's the lake!" he added, pointing.

Henry ran down to the water's edge. Peter followed. The embankment narrowed to a point. Peter **slipped** past Henry and bagged the best spot, right at the water's edge where the ducks gathered.

"Hey, get away from there," said Henry.

"I want to feed the ducks," said Peter.

"I want to feed the ducks,"
said Henry. "Now move."

"I was here first," said Peter.

"Not any more," said Henry.

Horrid Henry *pushed* Peter.

"Out of my way, **worm!**"

Perfect Peter pushed him back.

"Don't call me worm!"

Henry wobbled.

Peter wobbled.

Splash!

Peter tumbled into the lake.

Crash!

Henry tumbled into the lake.

"My babies!" shrieked Mum, jumping in after them.

"My – **glug glug glug**!" shrieked Dad, jumping into the muddy water after her.

"My new wellies!" gurgled Perfect Peter.

BANG!

Pow!

Terminator Gladiator slashed at

Rapper Zapper.

ZAP!

Rapper Zapper slashed back.

"**GO, Zappy!**" yelled Henry, lying

bundled up in blankets on the sofa.

Once everyone had scrambled out of

the lake, Mum and Dad had been keen to get home as fast as possible.

"I think the park next time," mumbled Dad, sneezing.

"Definitely," mumbled Mum, coughing.

"Oh, I don't know," said Horrid Henry happily. "A little water never hurt anyone."

HORRID HENRY'S
SWIMMING LESSON

Oh no! thought Horrid Henry. He pulled the duvet tightly over his head.

It was Thursday. **HORRIBLE, HORRIBLE THURSDAY**. The worst day of the week. Horrid Henry was certain Thursdays came more often than any other day.

Thursday was his class *swimming* day. Henry had a nagging feeling that this Thursday was even **WORSE** than all the other **AWFUL** Thursdays.

Thursday
June 22

Horrid Henry liked the bus ride to the pool. Horrid Henry liked doing the dance of the seven towels in the changing room. He also liked **HIDING** in the lockers, *throwing* socks in the pool and **splashing** everyone.

The only thing Henry didn't like about **GOING** swimming was . . .

SWIMMING.

The truth was, Horrid Henry hated water. **UGGGH!** Water was so . . . **wet!** And *soggy*. The chlorine *stung* his eyes. He never knew what **horrors** might be lurking in the deep end. And the pool was so **cold** penguins could fly in for the winter.

Fortunately, Henry had a *brilliant* list of excuses. He'd pretend he had a **verruca**, or a *tummy ache*, or had lost his swimming costume.

Unfortunately, the **MEAN**, **NASTY**, **HORRIBLE** swimming teacher, Soggy Sid, usually made him get in the pool anyway.

Then Henry would **DUCK** Dizzy Dave, or **splash** Weepy William, or **PINCH** Gorgeous Gurinder, until Sid ordered him out. It was not surprising that Horrid Henry had never managed to get his five-metre badge.

ARRRGH! Now he remembered. Today was test day. The **terrible** day when everyone had to show how far they could swim. Aerobic Al was going for gold. Moody Margaret was going for SILVER. The only ones who were still trying for their five-metre badges were Lazy Linda and Horrid Henry. FIVE WHOLE METRES! How could anyone swim such a vast distance?

If only they were tested on who could S_I_N_K to the bottom of the pool the fastest, or **splash** the most, or spit water the furthest, then Horrid Henry would have every badge in a jiffy. But no. He had to leap into a **FREEZING COLD POOL**, and, if he survived that shock, somehow thrash his way across five whole metres without drowning.

Well, there was **NO WAY** he was going to school today.

Mum came into his room.

"I can't go to school today, Mum," Henry moaned. "I feel **terrible**."

Mum didn't even look at him.

"**THURSDAY-ITIS** again, I presume," said Mum.

"No way!" said Henry. "I didn't even know it was Thursday."

"Get up, Henry," said Mum. "You're going swimming and that's that."

Perfect Peter peeked round the door.

"It's badge day today!" he said. "I'm going for fifty metres!"

"That's **brilliant**, Peter," said Mum. "I bet you're the best swimmer in your class."

Perfect Peter smiled modestly.

"I just try my best," he said. "Good luck with your five-metre badge, Henry," he added.

Horrid Henry **GROWLED** and **attacked**. He was a **VENUS FLYTRAP** slowly mashing a frantic fly between his deadly leaves.

"Eeeeeowwwww!" screeched Peter.

"Stop being **horrid**, Henry!"
screamed Mum. "Leave your poor
brother alone!"

Horrid Henry let Peter go. If
only he could find some way not to

take his swimming test he'd be the
happiest boy in the world.

Henry's class arrived at the pool.
Right, thought Henry. Time to
unpack his excuses to Soggy Sid.

"I can't go swimming, I've got a
verruca," lied Henry.

"**TAKE OFF YOUR SOCK**," ordered
Soggy Sid.

RATS, thought Henry.

"Maybe it's better now," said Henry.

"I thought so," said Sid.

Horrid Henry grabbed his stomach.

"**Tummy pains!**" he moaned. "I feel terrible."

"You seemed fine when you were prancing round the pool a moment ago," snapped Sid. "**NOW GET CHANGED.**"

Time for the **KILLER EXCUSE**.

"I forgot my swimming costume!" said Henry. This was his best chance of success.

"No problem," said Soggy Sid. He handed Henry a bag. "Put on one of these."

SLOWLY, Horrid Henry rummaged in

the bag. He pulled out a bikini top,
a blue costume with a **HOLE** in the
middle, a pair of pink pants, a TINY
pair of green trunks, a polka-dot
one-piece with bunnies, see-through
white shorts, and a nappy.

"I can't wear any of these!"
protested Horrid Henry.

"YOU CAN AND YOU WILL, IF I HAVE TO PUT THEM ON YOU MYSELF," snarled Sid.

Horrid Henry SQUEEZED into the green trunks. He could barely breathe. Slowly, he joined the rest of his class *pushing* and **shoving** by the side of the pool.

Everyone had **MILLIONS** of badges sewn all over their costumes. You couldn't even see Aerobic Al's bathing suit beneath the stack of badges.

"**HEY YOU!**" shouted Soggy

184

Sid. He pointed at Weepy William.

"Where's your swimming costume?"

Weepy William glanced down and **burst** into tears.

"WAAAAAH," he wailed, and ran weeping back to the changing room.

"**NOW GET IN!**" ordered Soggy Sid.

"**BUT I'LL DROWN!**" screamed Henry. "**I CAN'T SWIM!**"

"**GET IN!**" screamed Soggy Sid.

Goodbye, cruel world. Horrid Henry held his breath and fell into the icy water. **ARRRRGH!** He was turning

into an iceberg!

He was **DYING!** He was **DEAD!** His feet flailed madly as he sank

DOWN,
DOWN,
DOWN
– clunk!

Henry's feet touched the bottom. Henry stood up, **CHOKING** and **spluttering**. He was waist-deep in water.

"LINDA AND HENRY! SWIM FIVE METRES - NOW!"

What am I going to do? thought Henry. It was so humiliating not even being able to swim five metres! Everyone would **TEASE** him. And he'd have to listen to them **bragging** about their badges! Wouldn't it be great to get a badge? Somehow?

Lazy Linda set off, VERY VERY SLOWLY. Horrid Henry grabbed on to her leg. Maybe she'll pull me across, he thought.

"UGGGH!" gurgled Lazy Linda.

"LEAVE HER ALONE!" shouted Sid.

"LAST CHANCE, HENRY."

Horrid Henry ran along the pool's bottom and *flapped* his arms, pretending to swim.

"Did it!" said Henry.

Soggy Sid scowled.

"I SAID SWIM, NOT WALK!" screamed Sid. "You've failed. Now

get over to the far lane and practise. Remember, anyone who stops swimming during the test doesn't get a badge."

Horrid Henry **stomped** over to the far lane. No way was he going to practise! **HOW HE HATED SWIMMING!** He watched the others splashing **UP** and **DOWN**, **UP** and **DOWN**. There was Aerobic Al, doing his laps like a **bolt of lightning**. And **MOODY MARGARET**. And Kung-Fu Kate. Everyone would be getting a badge but Henry. It was so unfair.

"**PSSST, SUSAN**," said Henry. "Have you

heard? There's a **SHARK** in the deep end!"

"Oh yeah, right," said Sour Susan. She looked at the **DARK** water in the far end of the pool.

"Don't believe me," said Henry. "Find out the hard way. Come back with a leg missing."

Sour Susan paused and WHISPERED

something to Moody Margaret.

"**SHUT UP, HENRY**," said Margaret.
They swam off.

"Don't worry about the shark,
Andrew," said Henry. "I think he's
already eaten today."

"**WHAT SHARK?**" said Anxious
Andrew.

Andrew stared at the deep end. It did look awfully dark down there.

"Start swimming, Andrew!" shouted Soggy Sid.

"I don't want to," said Andrew.

"Swim! Or I'll BITE you myself!" snarled Sid.

Andrew started swimming.

"Dave, Ralph, Clare and Bert — start swimming!" bellowed Soggy Sid.

"Look out for the **SHARK!**" said Horrid Henry. He watched Aerobic Al tearing up and down the lane.

"GOTTA SWIM, GOTTA SWIM, GOTTA SWIM,"

muttered Al between strokes.

What a show-off, thought Henry. Wouldn't it be fun to play a TRICK on him?

Horrid Henry pretended he was a CROCODILE. He sneaked under the water to the middle of the pool and waited until Aerobic Al swam overhead. Then Horrid Henry reached up.

PINCH! Henry grabbed Al's thrashing leg.

"**AAAARGGGH!**" screamed Al. "Something's grabbed my leg. Help!"

Aerobic Al leapt out of the pool.

Tee hee, thought Horrid Henry.

"**IT'S A SHARK!**" screamed
Sour Susan. She scrambled out of the
pool.

"**THERE'S A SHARK IN THE POOL!**"
screeched Anxious Andrew.

"**There's a shark in the pool!**"

howled Rude Ralph.

Everyone was screaming and shouting and struggling to get out.

The only one left in the pool was Henry.

shark!

Horrid Henry forgot there were no *sharks* in swimming pools.

Horrid Henry forgot *he'd* started the shark rumour.

Horrid Henry forgot he couldn't swim.

All he knew was that he was alone
in the pool – **WITH A SHARK!**
Horrid Henry swam for his life.
SHAKING and QUAKING, **splashing** and

crashing, he torpedoed his way to the side of the pool and scrambled out. He gasped and panted. Thank goodness. Safe at last! He'd never ever go swimming again.

"**FIVE METRES!**" bellowed Soggy Sid. "You've all failed your badges today, except for — Henry!"

"*WAAAAAAAHHHHHH!*" wailed the other children.

"**whoopee!**" **screamed Henry. "Olympics, here I come!**"

HORRID HENRY

HOLIDAY HORRORS

Turn the page for some horribly fun games and activities!

Spot-the-Difference

HORRID HENRY LOVES HOIDAYS BUT HE'S NOT ALWAYS THE BEST BEHAVED ON THEM. SPOT THE SIX DIFFERENCES IN THE IMAGE OF HENRY CAUSING HAVOC BELOW.

HINT:
WHAT'S
HENRY
WEARING?

FREE

Athletic Crossword

HELP HENRY LEARN ALL ABOUT THE OLYMPICS WITH
THIS TRICKY CROSSWORD.

ACROSS

1. EVERYONE WANTS TO WIN THESE
6. THESE GO ON YOUR FEET TO HELP YOU RUN
9. THIS PERSON HELPS THE ATHLETES TRAIN FOR THE GAMES
10. YOU THROW THIS LONG, POINTY STICK

DOWN

2. YOU MUST WEAR THIS IN THE POOL
3. IT HAS TWO WHEELS AND HANDLEBARS
4. JUMP OVER THESE TO WIN THE RACE
5. YOU KICK THIS BLACK AND WHITE BALL
7. YOU NEED ONE OF THESE TO HIT THE TENNIS BALL
8. ONLY THE BRAVEST JUMP OFF THE TOP BOARD

chicken Run

HENRY'S CLASS CHICKEN HAS GOT OUT OF HER PEN. HELP HENRY CATCH HER BY FINDING THE QUICKEST ROUTE THROUGH THE MAZE.

Perfect Peter's Perfect Holiday Quiz

PERFECT PETER HAS CREATED A QUIZ TO HELP YOU DECIDE
WHERE TO GO ON HOLIDAY. ANSWER THE QUESTIONS
BELOW TO FIND OUT YOUR PERFECT VACATION SPOT!

1. *When you hear you're going on holiday, you are …*
   a. Excited! Better grab my sunglasses
   b. Ready for adventure! Where are my trainers? ✓
   c. Miserable! I HATE packing!

2. *Your favourite time of year is …*
   a. Summer
   b. Spring ✓
   c. Autumn ✓

3. *Your go-to holiday essentials are …*
   a. Flip flops and a beach ball ✓
   b. A fishing rod and board games
   c. A TV and lots of snacks!

4. *The first thing you do on holiday is …*
   a. Go for a swim
   b. Go for a walk ✓
   c. Go for a nap ✓

5. *Your favourite drink by the pool is …*
   a. Something fruity with a little umbrella ✓
   b. Water – got to keep hydrated!
   c. Fizzy drinks, the fizzier the better!

6. *In the evenings you often …*
   a. Watch a TV show with my family ✓
   b. Play board games with my friends
   c. Watch scary movies on my own (NO BABIES ALLOWED!)

7. *You travel to your destination by …*
   a. Plane
   b. Train /
   c. Car ✓

8. *The worst day of the holiday is when …*
   a. You get sunburnt. OW!
   b. You have to leave! ✓
   c. EVERY DAY!

9. *Your favourite thing to do on holiday is …*
   a. Build sandcastles ✓
   b. Explore the woods ✓
   c. Read comic books

10. *You prefer to stay in …*
    a. A hotel
    b. A tent
    c. Your own bed ✓

MOSTLY A
The beach!
Your ideal holiday has sun, sea and sand! Time to pack your swimsuit and head to the beach.

MOSTLY C
Staying at home!
You HATE packing for a holiday and would much rather stay inside and watch TV. Going on holiday sucks!

MOSTLY B
Camping!
You love to spend time outdoors so camping is perfect for you. Don't forget to pack the marshmallows to toast on the fire – yum!

Sizzling Sudoku

IT'S BEEN A LONG, HOT SUMMER BUT BEFORE AEROBIC
AL AND HORRID HENRY CAN COOL OFF IN THE POOL THEY
HAVE TO COMPLETE THESE TRICKY SUDOKUS.

				7	1	4		3
	3	7	6	5			8	
4	5					7		9
6			8	1	3	2	7	5
		5	4			8	3	
1			7	2	5		9	4
3			2	4			1	
				3	8			
	2				9	3	4	

Ru[...]

NOW FOR AN EVEN TRICKIER ONE!

9		4		1	2	7		8
2	7		6	9			5	
	6		4	5	7	2		
3	1	6	2	4		8		5
8	2		5	6				3
	9		7	8	3	1	2	6
				6				
5	8	2		3	4	6	9	
6	4	9			5			2

Rude Ralph's Rude Jokes

RUDE RALPH LOVES TO THINK UP RUDE JOKES.
HAVE YOU HEARD ANY OF THESE BEFORE?

Why did the tomato blush?

Because he saw the salad dressing.

What do you call a dog magician?

A Labracadabrador.

Why did the student eat his homework?

Because his teacher said it would be a piece of cake.

What did one toilet say to another toilet?

You look a bit flushed!

How do you know if a vampire has a cold?

They start coffin.

What did the left eye say to the right eye?

Between us, something smells!

Why was six afraid of seven?

Because seven *eight* nine!

What did the nose say to the finger?

Quit picking on me!

How do you talk to a giant?
Use big words!

Why did the dinosaur refuse to wear deodorant?

He didn't want to be EX-STINK!

clever clare's Brain Teasers

CLEVER CLARE HAS ALREADY FINISHED ALL HER HOLIDAY HOMEWORK SO SHE'S CREATED SOME BRAIN TEASERS TO TRY ON HER FRIENDS. HOW MANY CAN YOU GET RIGHT?

1. PEOPLE MAKE ME, SAVE ME, CHANGE ME, RAISE ME. WHAT AM I?

2. WHAT HAS A FACE AND TWO HANDS BUT NO ARMS OR LEGS?

3. WHY ARE GHOSTS BAD AT LYING?

4. WHAT TYPE OF CHEESE IS MADE BACKWARDS?

5. I TURN ONCE AND WHAT IS OUT WILL NOT GET IN. I TURN AGAIN AND WHAT IS IN WILL NOT GET OUT. WHAT AM I?

6. WHAT HAS TO BE BROKEN BEFORE YOU CAN EAT IT?

7. I COME DOWN, BUT I NEVER GO UP. WHAT AM I?

8. I AM FULL OF HOLES BUT I CAN STILL HOLD A LOT OF WATER. WHAT AM I?

9. WHAT HAS A HEAD AND A TAIL BUT NO BODY?

10. YOU CAN CATCH ME, BUT YOU CAN'T THROW ME. WHAT AM I?

who's who?

DO YOU THINK YOU KNOW ALL THE HORRID HENRY CHARACTERS? MATCH THE CHARACTERS TO THEIR SILHOUETTES.

DAD

HORRID HENRY

MUM

PERFECT PETER

SOUR SUSAN

RUDE RALPH

MISS BATTLE-AXE

MOODY MARGARET

Make Your Own Secret Den

WANT TO KNOW HOW TO MAKE YOUR OWN HIDE-OUT JUST LIKE HENRY'S? FOLLOW THESE EASY STEPS TO HAVE YOUR OWN SUPER COOL SECRET DEN!

YOU WILL NEED:

- CUSHIONS • BLANKETS • SHEETS
- PEGS • A CARDBOARD BOX • SOME CHAIRS

1. Pick the perfect spot in your house for your den. Is it going to be in your bedroom or the living room?

2. Gather all the cushions, blankets and sheets you can carry.

3. Use the sofa or your bed, and some chairs to build the walls of your den.

4. Cover the tops of the chairs with sheets and use the pegs to hold them in place.

5. Fill the space under the sheets with blankets and cushions. You want it to be nice and cosy!

6. Take your box and fill it with your favourite snacks. Now, hide it in your den so Perfect Peter won't find it!

7. Gather all of your favourite toys, books and a torch and have fun in your brand new den!

BONUS STEP:
Make up a secret password or handshake for visitors to your den. No snivelling babies allowed!

Plane Food

HENRY LOVES GOING ON PLANES BUT HE HATES PLANE FOOD! HELP HIM FIND THE TASTY TREATS AMONGST THE FOOD ITEMS BELOW BY CIRCLING HENRY'S FAVOURITE FOODS. REMEMBER HE LOVES SWEETS, FIZZY DRINKS AND ANY JUNK FOOD HE CAN GET HIS HANDS ON.

Weepy William's Would You Rather

WEEPY WILLIAM HAS WRITTEN SOME "WOULD YOU RATHER" QUESTIONS FOR PERFECT PETER BUT IT LOOKS LIKE HORRID HENRY HAS CHANGED SOME OF THEM. WHY NOT ASK YOUR FRIENDS THESE QUESTIONS AND SEE IF YOU CAN GUESS WHICH ONES HENRY WROTE.

fly

1. Would you rather be able to fly or be invisible?

2. Would you rather jump into a pool of custard or a pool of strawberry ice cream? *custard*

3. Would you rather throw water balloons at *water balloons* Moody Margaret or pull Sour Susan's hair?

4. Would you rather help Mum hoover the house or Dad unpack the shopping? *unpack* *Shopping*

5. Would you rather go on the biggest roller *Car* coaster in the world or drive the fastest car?

6. Would you rather eat a dead spider or a live worm? *Spider* *Spider*

Swimming Race!

HORRID HENRY HAS CHALLENGED MOODY MARGARET
AND AEROBIC AL TO A SWIMMING RACE. WHICH ONE OF
THEM WINS? FOLLOW THE LINES TO FIND OUT.

Moody Margaret   Aerobic Al   Horrid Henry

FINISH

school's out

IT'S THE FIRST DAY OF THE SCHOOL HOLIDAYS AND
INSTEAD OF HAVING THE TV ALL TO HIMSELF,
HENRY'S CLASSMATES HAVE COME ROUND TO WATCH
A MOVIE. COLOUR IN THE FRIENDS WATCHING TV.

ANSWERS

Spot-the-Difference

Athletic crossword

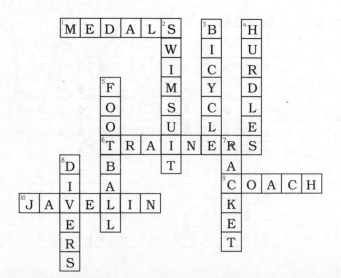

chicken Run

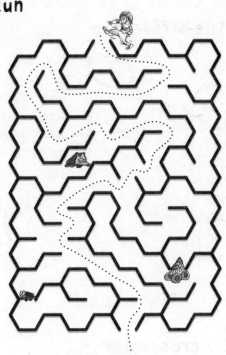

Sizzling Sudoku

8	6	2	9	7	1	4	5	3
9	3	7	6	5	4	1	8	2
4	5	1	3	8	2	7	6	9
6	4	9	8	1	3	2	7	5
2	7	5	4	9	6	8	3	1
1	8	3	7	2	5	6	9	4
3	9	6	2	4	7	5	1	8
7	1	4	5	3	8	9	2	6
5	2	8	1	6	9	3	4	7

9	5	4	3	1	2	7	6	8
2	7	3	6	9	8	4	5	1
1	6	8	4	5	7	2	3	9
3	1	6	2	4	9	8	7	5
8	2	7	5	6	1	9	4	3
4	9	5	7	8	3	1	2	6
7	3	1	9	2	6	5	8	4
5	8	2	1	3	4	6	9	7
6	4	9	8	7	5	3	1	2

clever clare's Brain Teasers

1. MONEY
2. A CLOCK
3. YOU CAN SEE RIGHT THROUGH THEM
4. EDAM
5. A KEY
6. AN EGG
7. RAIN
8. A SPONGE
9. A COIN
10. A COLD

who's who?

A. DAD
B. SOUR SUSAN
C. RUDE RALPH
D. MOODY MARGARET
E. HORRID HENRY
F. PERFECT PETER
G. MISS BATTLE-AXE
H. MUM

Plane Food

Weepy William's Would You Rather

HORRID HENRY WROTE QUESTIONS 3, 5 AND 6.

Swimming Race!

Moody Margaret   Aerobic Al   Horrid Henry

FINISH

Aerobic Al wins!

COLLECT ALL THE
HORRID HENRY STORYBOOKS!